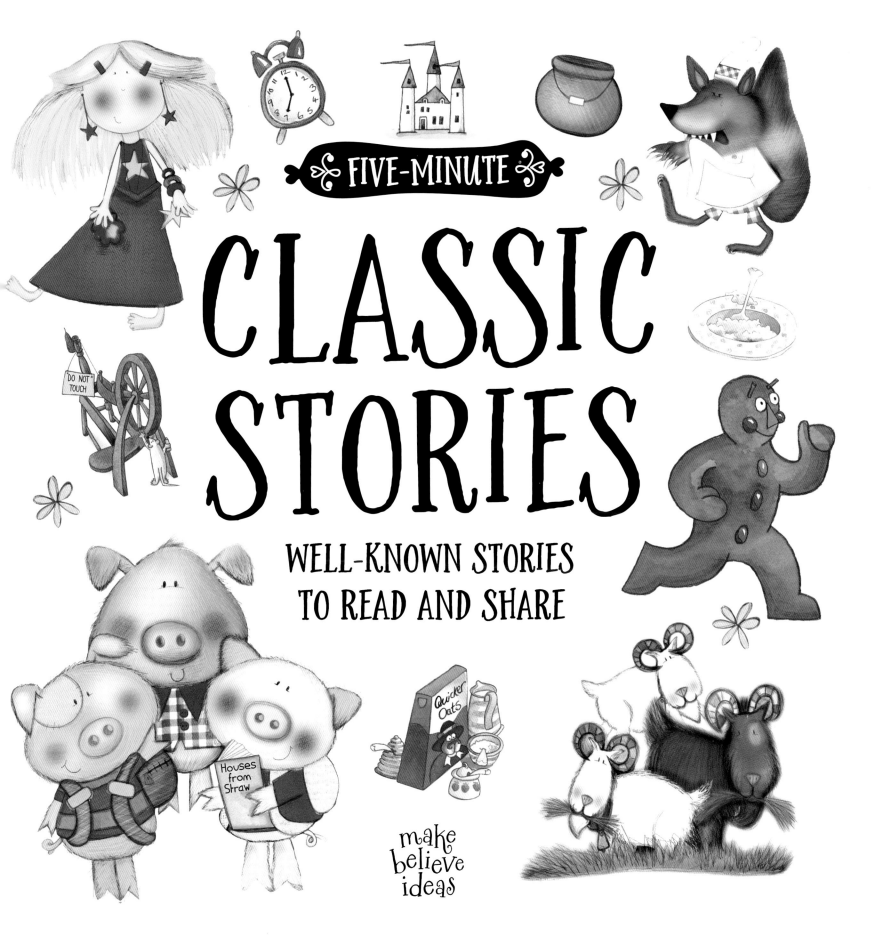

FIVE-MINUTE
CLASSIC STORIES

WELL-KNOWN STORIES TO READ AND SHARE

make
believe
ideas

Here are some fairy tales written in rhyme.
We think they're perfect for you at bedtime.
There's something else – can you guess what?
Throughout each story, there's an object to spot.

STORIES RETOLD BY NICK AND CLAIRE PAGE

·

ILLUSTRATED BY SARA BAKER AND KATIE SAUNDERS

✳ CONTENTS ✳

Search for these objects in the stories.

The Elves and the Shoemaker

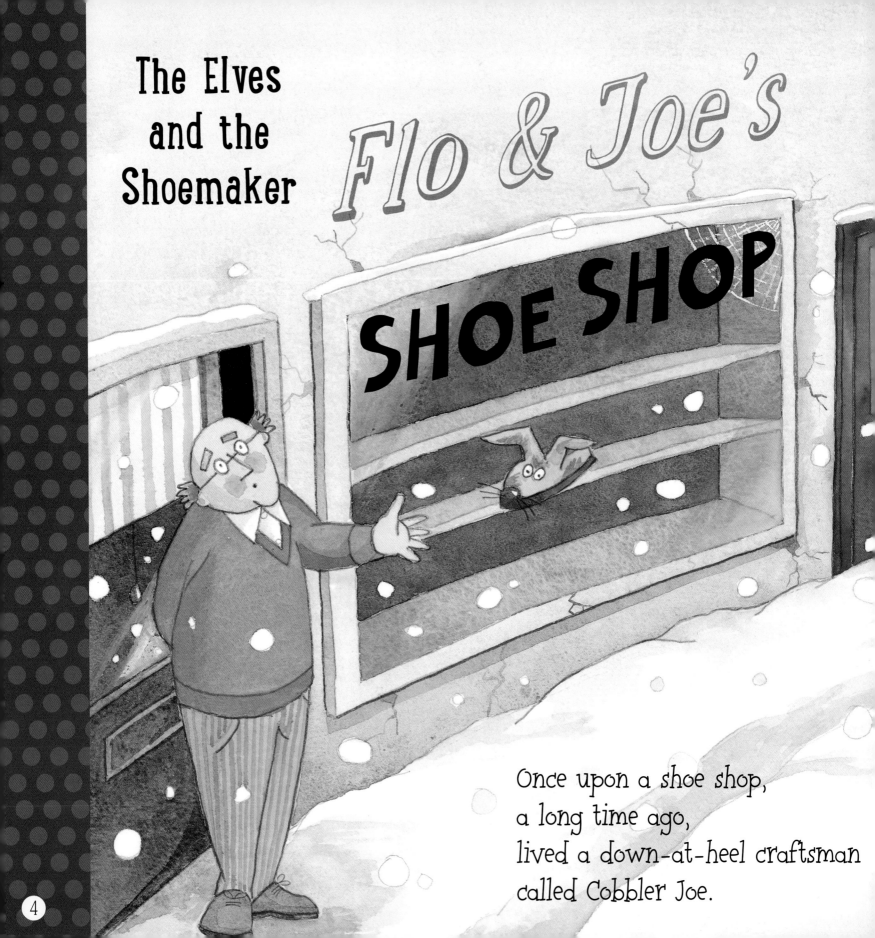

Once upon a shoe shop,
a long time ago,
lived a down-at-heel craftsman
called Cobbler Joe.

Heel and toe, stitch and sew,
making boots and shoes to go!
Very tired and hungry was poor old Cobbler Joe.
"There is nothing left to eat!" declared his wife, Flo.

Joe was sad. Things were bad.
Just some leather was all they had.

He cut a piece of leather,
enough for one small pair,
laid it on his workbench, and left it there.
Shook his head, went to bed.
"Start on them tomorrow," old Joe said.

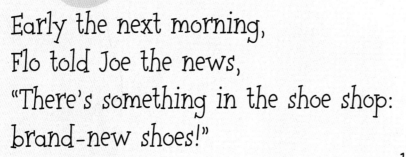

Early the next morning,
Flo told Joe the news,
"There's something in the shoe shop:
brand-new shoes!"

Heel and toe,
stitch and sew,
someone's done
the work for Joe!

Joe put them in the window –
can you guess what?
A lady came and bought them;
she paid a lot!
Said she, "I'll tell high and low:
buy your shoes from Flo and Joe!"

Joe and Flo had money –
and no time to lose,
they bought some fine leather
to make more shoes.
"Cut it right, leave in sight,
will it happen again tonight?"

Star
Buy

WATCH THIS
SPACE

Joe and Flo next morning, what did they behold?
TWO new pairs of boots there, waiting to be sold!

They were beauties. They were cuties.
Joe and Flo sold both those booties!

NEW STYLES *delivered* • EACH • NIGHT •

Every night, this happened, just the same.
When Joe left out the leather, new shoes came.

Sew and stitch, not a hitch,
Flo and Joe got very rich!

On Christmas Eve, at teatime, Flo said to Joe,
"Let's wait up and find out who helps us sew."
So they hid, eyes open wide.
What surprises there they spied!

As the clock chimed midnight,
singing to themselves,
there appeared, with toolbags,
two small elves.
Tip tap here,
tip tap there,
working in their
underwear!

GLUE

SHOE MAKING

13

Two elves with no clothes on,
working in the shop!
Sunrise came,
they downed their tools,
and off they hopped.
Heel and toe,
stitch and sew.
"We must make them
clothes!" said Flo.

Joe and Flo made outfits, left them on the table,
in boxes tied with ribbon and a label:

"Now we know!
Thank you so.
To our friends,
love, Joe and Flo!"

When the clock struck midnight,
Joe and Flo looked on.
The elves unwrapped their outfits,
put them on!

"What a day! It's our pay!
Now we can be on our way!"

And that's where all this ended. The elves went away.
But Joe and Flo were rich now, so that was all okay.

Heel and toe, Flo and Joe,
once upon a shoe shop,
a long time ago.

The Little Mermaid

In a beautiful palace,
under the sea,
lived a mermaid princess
who was called Coralie.
As she played with the gulls,
one grey, windy dawn,
she saw a small boat
that was caught in a storm.

Prince Roderick was fishing for pearls in the sea,
when a wave hit the boat!
He fell in, "Quick! Help me!"
She rescued the prince, brought him safe to the bay,
sang softly to wake him and then swam away.

Back at the palace, her head was in a whirl,
"I wish – how I wish – that I was a girl!"
Her sisters, called Laura and Flora and Dora,
said, "Why don't you go to see Seaweedy Nora?"

Now Nora was smelly and not very nice.
She liked to eat jellyfish, sea slugs and lice.

At the back of her cave,
deep down in the ocean,
Seaweedy Nora
mixed up a dark potion.

Seaweedy
Nora →

Nora said, "Here, I can give you your wish. Drink this and you'll be a lot less like a fish. Now pay me by filling this shell with your voice!" So Coralie paid – there was simply no choice.

She drank up the drink (it smelled of fish eggs),
and when she reached land, her tail became legs!

Later, Prince Roderick sailed past her once more
and said to her, "Haven't I seen you before?"

But she couldn't speak, so she looked into his eyes.
She stepped into the boat, and to her surprise,
the prince leaned towards her, to give her a kiss.
But Seaweedy Nora said, "I must stop this!"

With Coralie's voice, she sang,
"Prince, come to me!"
and the prince, now enchanted,
jumped into the sea!

Coralie watched but could
not say a word.
Then, on a rock near her,
she spotted a bird.

The bird went and fetched
all of Coralie's friends –
seagulls and crabs
and a lobster called Ben.
They pecked at old Nora
and broke the seashell.
Coralie's voice was released –
they had broken the spell!

Seaweedy Nora was chased far away,
and the prince and the mermaid were married that day.
Now the mermaid's a girl, Coralie has her wish –
but sometimes she wishes that she was a fish!

The Gingerbread Man

There once was a little old baker
and a little old baker's wife.
One day, they baked a gingerbread man,
who magically came to life!

The name that they gave him was Gingerbread Fred.
And they said, "Don't go out on the street!
You are not a real boy; you're a biscuit –
and that makes you yummy to eat!"

But before you could say
"JAMMY DOUGHNUTS",
their gingerbread son
had started to run!

And Gingerbread Fred said . . .

"Run, run, run, as fast as you can.
You can't catch me, I'm the gingerbread man!"

First, Gingerbread Fred reached a garden,
where a cat lay asleep in the flowers.
"MEE-WOW!" said the cat.
"Here comes breakfast! I've been
waiting for hours and hours!"

But Fred didn't wait –
he started to skate!

And Gingerbread Fred said . . .

"Skate, skate, skate,
as fast as you can.
You can't catch me,
I'm the gingerbread man!"

Next, Gingerbread Fred reached a farmyard,
where a dog lay asleep in the hay,
"BOW-WOW!" said the dog.
"It must be lunchtime!
It's a gingerbread-man takeaway!"

But before you could say,
"LEMON CHEESECAKE",
Fred turned aside
and started to ride!

And Gingerbread Fred said . . .

"Ride, ride, ride,
as fast as you can.
You can't catch me,
I'm the gingerbread man!"

34

Then Gingerbread Fred reached the river,
where a fox sat, watching the fish.
"Need some help?" said the fox.
"Jump on my back.
I can take you across, if you wish."

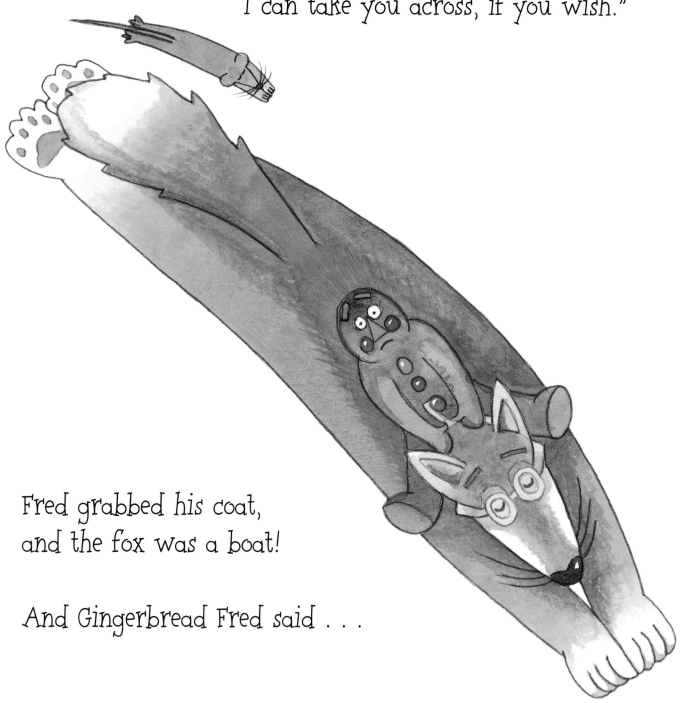

Fred grabbed his coat,
and the fox was a boat!

And Gingerbread Fred said . . .

"Swim, swim, swim, as fast as you can.
You can't catch me, I'm the gingerbread man!"

As the water gradually rose,
the fox said to Fred,
"Move up further.
It's best if you sit on my nose."

Quite soon, they were over the river,
and Gingerbread Fred said, "Goodbye!"
"Not so fast," said the fox.
"There's one more thing.
Now, how would you like to fly?"

And before you could say
"GINGER SNAPS",
Fred was thrown high up in the sky!

And Gingerbread Fred said . . .

"Fly, fly, fly,
as fast as you can.
You can't catch me,
I'm the . . ."

CRUNCH! SCRUNCH! MUNCH!
The fox had him for lunch.

And Gingerbread Fred
said nothing ever again.

Sleeping Beauty

Once a king and queen
held a party on the green,
to celebrate their baby.
They called her Crystal Clean.

They were thrilled to bits!
The king did the splits.
The queen served lots of crackers
with cheese and other bits.

Among the many guests
to welcome the princess
were seven kindly fairies,
who came with presents to bless.

A scary fairy came.
Griselda was her name.
She hadn't been invited
but walked in all the same.

"A curse!" Griselda said.
"A curse upon her head!
She'll be pricked by a spindle.
Your baby will be dead!"

"No need for any fears,"
the youngest fairy cheered.
"I'll change this curse, instead
she will sleep for a hundred years."

The queen warned Crystal Clean,
each year till age sixteen,
"Don't ever touch a spindle.
You don't know where it's been."

But then one night,
to her delight,
the princess found a tower,
and there, shining bright
a spinning wheel she found,
spinning round and round.
She pricked her little finger
and fell to the ground.

You couldn't hear a peep.
Everybody fell asleep.
The place was filled with snoring
and everyone was dreaming deep.

A hundred years went by. The ivy climbed so high, you'd never know the castle stood nearby.

Then along the forest floor, came a prince, who found the door. He cut through thorns and roses and thought he heard a snore.

The castle was in a mess,
but the prince found the princess.
He fell in love, he kissed her,
and she woke up! Success!

He married Crystal Clean,
and on the village green
they held the biggest party
that you've ever seen!

Three Billy Goats Gruff

In the valley, by a river,
lived three happy billy goats.
One was small: Little Will,
with a bell around his throat.
One was tall: Brother Bill,
with a big and shaggy coat.
One was HUGE: Rough Tough Gruff.
He could turn you into fluff!

On the mountain, by a bridge,
lived a nasty troll called Sid.
He had eyes big as pies,
ears like two big saucepan lids,
yellow teeth, wrinkly throat
and his favourite food was goat!

In the valley, one fine day,
there was not much grass around.
"Time to go," said Little Will.
"Let's climb up to higher ground.
Cross the bridge, to the pass
where there's loads of lovely grass!"

Stay off or else.
No trespassing

So the three goats trotted off
to the bridge up by the pass.
"I'll go first," said Little Will.
"Look at all that lovely grass."
Trip-trap-trip! As he ran,
Sid the Troll jumped out and sang . . .

"Don't want chicken,
don't want lamb,
don't want bacon,
don't want ham.

Don't want turkey or beef or pork.
Want some goat upon my fork!"

Little Will sweetly smiled, and he gave a little bleat.
"Don't have me for your tea; I am not much good to eat.
But if goat is your prize, why not try some Goat Surprise?"

"Goat Surprise?" said the troll.
"Oooh, that sounds completely yummy!"
"Just you wait," said Little Will,
"and you'll have some in your tummy.
My big bro' can tell you more
about this meal so scrummy.
Let me through, if you will."
And he crossed onto the hill.

Brother Bill came along
with his great big shaggy coat.
Trip-trap-trip! As he ran,
Sid the Troll jumped out and sang . . .

"Don't want apples,
don't want cherries.
Don't want plums or grapes or prunes.
Want some goat upon my spoon!"

Brother Bill calmly stood,
and he gave a little baa.
"Don't have me for your tea;
eating me won't get you far.
But to fill your insides,
you should try some Goat Surprise."

"Goat Surprise?" said the troll.
"Ooooh! Sounds absolutely great!"
"In a mo'," said Brother Bill,
"you will have some on your plate!
My big brother will be here.
All you have to do is wait.
Let me through; let me pass."
And he went to eat some grass.

Rough Tough Gruff soon appeared,
and up to the bridge he sped.
He was huge; he was fierce,
with great horns upon his head.
Trip-trap-trip! As he ran,
Sid the Troll jumped out and sang . . .

"Don't want lettuce, don't want beans,
don't want cabbage, don't want greens.
Don't want carrots, peas or shallots!
Want some goat here in my pot!"

Rough Tough Gruff just stood still,
and he said to Sid the Troll,
"If it's goat that you want,
you can put me in your bowl.
Pick on someone your own size!
Here's my special Goat Surprise!"

"Goat Surprise?" cried the troll. "Ooooh, it's come my way at last!"
Then he saw Rough Tough Gruff charging straight for him, fast!
Sid felt sick, when a kick hit him like a mighty blast.
Rough Tough Gruff put Sid in plaster.
Then he went to munch some pasture.

Those three goats set up home, on that green and grassy hill.
With a munch they had their lunch,
Rough Tough Gruff and Bill and Will.
Sid the Troll disappeared; all his friends said he was ill.
From then on, you will note,
he couldn't stand the taste of goat.

Do not enter

Three Little Pigs

Three little pigs left home one day,
packed their bags and went on their way.
Mother Pig said, "Goodbye, bye, bye!"
But a wolf saw them go and thought,
"Mmm – PORK PIE!"

The first little pig met a man selling straw.
"Will it make a good house? I'm not quite sure."
Then he paid for the bales and stacked them high,
but the wolf licked his lips, thinking,
"Mmm – STIR-FRY!"

The second little pig met a man selling wood.
"I think I'll build with this; it looks quite good."
So he worked all day and did not stop,
but the wolf licked his lips, thinking,
"Mmm – PORK CHOP!"

The third little pig met a man selling bricks.
"These look strong, much better than sticks."
So he built his house, all shiny and new,
but the wolf licked his lips, thinking,
"Mmm – BARBECUE!"

When each home was complete,
they went inside for something to eat.
But the wolf was feeling hungry, too,
and he licked his lips, thinking,
"Mmm – PORK STEW!"

Mr Wolf's top ten pork dishes

Said the wolf to Piggy Straw, "Now let me in!"
"Not by the hair on my chinny chin chin!"
So the wolf huffed and puffed,
and the house went WHAM!
And the wolf licked his lips, shouting,
"Mmm – BOILED HAM!"

Piggy Straw ran straight to the house of Piggy Wood.
And behind him came the wolf, "Let me in! I'll be good!"

Then he huffed and he puffed,
and the house went SMASH!
And the wolf licked his lips, shouting,
"Mmm – GOULASH!"

Then the two pigs ran to the house made of bricks.
They were chased by the wolf (who was not quite as quick).

There he huffed and he puffed,
but the house stayed whole.
So the wolf climbed the roof,
shouting, "Mmm – CASSEROLE!"

No Salesmen
No Wolves
Please!

No
Wolves

Then the three pigs ran,
and they fetched a pot.
"Quick, quick," said Piggy Bricks,
"let's make it hot!"
As the hungry wolf jumped
down the chimney tower,
he landed in the pot and screamed,
"Oww – SWEET AND SOUR!"

He jumped out quick and ran far away
from the bricks, the wood and the pile of hay.

And the lesson of this story is –
learn it quick –
don't be a silly sausage –
make your house out of bricks!

Goldilocks and the Three Bears

In a house in the woods lives Daddy Bear,
married to Mum with curly hair.
Smallest of all, in the rocking chair,
is their baby, Little Bear Bottom.

It's breakfast time, believe it or not!
The porridge is done, but it's way too hot!
So they go for a walk, while it cools in the pot –
Mum, Dad and Little Bear Bottom.

Along comes a girl called Goldilocks,
wearing her favourite red and blue socks.
She walks straight in – the girl never knocks!
Her manners are gone – she forgot 'em!

She looks for some porridge, and, guess what!
One's too cold, and one's too hot.
The last is just right; she gobbles the lot.
What a bad little girl – she's rotten!

Feeling full up, she wants to sit down.
"Too hard! Too soft!" she says with a frown.
Tries baby bear's chair and ends upside down!
Crash! She's gone through the bottom!

Sleepy, she goes upstairs to bed.
Too high, too low; two beds hurt her head.
So she picks the little bear's bed instead.
(She likes the sheets – they are cotton.)

The bears come home. The bears are mad!
"Someone's been eating my porridge," says Dad.
"Mine too," says Mum,
"And mine," says their lad.
"She's eaten it right to the bottom!"

"Someone's been sitting here
in my chair," says Dad.
"And in my chair, too," Mum adds.
"My chair is broken.
Oh, I feel so sad!" cries
Little Bear Bottom.

They race up the stairs, and hearing a knock,
Goldilocks suddenly wakes with a shock!
Little Bear screams, and she's up like a shot.
"There's the intruder – we've got 'im!"

Out of the window she jumps – and away!
She learns a lot about bears that day –
their beds, their chairs, and to stay far away
from the porridge of Little Bear Bottom!

Rumpelstiltskin

There once was a miller who lied to the king,
"I have a sweet daughter called Geraldine.
She turns yellow straw into gold with one spin!"

The king locked the girl in a room full of straw,
saying, "Spin me gold or you'll die, for sure."
Geraldine wept. Then guess what she saw?

From a door in the floor, a little man sprang.
"Spin straw into gold? Why, do it I can!
Give me your necklace, and I am your man!"

Geraldine promised, and so he sang,
"Yellow straw, threads of gold! Spinning magic now behold!"
The straw turned to gold, and he left through the trapdoor.

The king was delighted with his golden thread.
"Now spin this lot, too," he greedily said,
"in time for tomorrow, or off with your head!"

The miller's girl cried, "Oh, no! More straw."
Then out came the man from his magic trapdoor:
"Give me your ring, and I'll help once more."

Geraldine promised, and so he sang,
"Yellow straw, threads of gold! Spinning magic now behold!"

The straw turned to gold,
and he left through the trapdoor.

Said the king, "Here, have one last try!"
Then went off again, as the girl gave a sigh,
"I have nothing to pay with. I'll have to die!"

When the little man saw the straw in a pile,
he gave her a look both cunning and wild.
"Do it, I will, but I'll have your first child!"
Sadly, Geraldine promised.

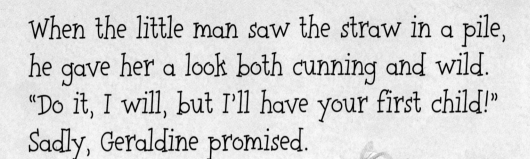

And so he sang:
"Yellow straw, threads of gold!
Spinning magic now behold!"
The straw turned to gold,
and he left through the trapdoor.

The girl married the king, had a baby next year,
and she'd almost forgotten the feeling of fear,
when from his trapdoor, the man reappeared.

"I've come for that baby,
asleep in the bed!"
"Not Gerald!" cried Geraldine.
"Take me instead!"
"I'll give you a test,"
the little man said.

"In three days at sunset, I'll visit again,
and give you a chance to guess my real name.
Get it wrong and the baby is mine all the same."
And he left through the door in the floor.

In three days the queen thought
her hopes were all shot,
but then a messenger cried.
"We've hit the jackpot!"

"In a house by the mountains, I saw a wee man,
shouting with glee at his wild, cunning plan.
Singing, 'Guess, she will not. Rumpelstiltskin I am!'"

That evening, as Geraldine poured some wine,
the little gold spinner appeared, right on time.
"Last chance!" he said. "Then the boy will be mine!
Or if it's too difficult, then just give in."

"Not so fast," said the queen. "Let the wheel have a spin.
Is it Boris? Or Britney? Or RUMPELSTILTSKIN?"

Rumpelstiltskin cried, "Noooooooo!"
Then he bounced round the room,
he swelled like a toad, and his head turned maroon.
And BANG! Rumpelstiltskin burst like a balloon!

Now the point of this story, we must say to you,
is: Don't ever lie about things you can't do.
Don't be greedy for gold, even if you're a king,
and never trust someone called . . .
RUMPELSTILTSKIN!